The Case of the Karate Chop

Book created by Parker C. Hinter

Written by Della Rowland

Illustrated by Diamond Studio

Based on characters from the Parker Brothers game

A Creative Media Applications Production

SCHOLASTIC INC.
New York Toronto London Auckland Sydney

ISBN 0-590-86635-4

Copyright © 1997 by Hasbro, Inc. All rights reserved. Published by Scholastic Inc. by arrangement with Parker Brothers, a division of Hasbro, Inc. CLUE ® is a registered trademark of Hasbro, Inc. for its detective game equipment.

12 11 10 9 8 7 6 5 4 3   7 8 9/9 0 1 2/0

Printed in the U.S.A.   40

First Scholastic printing, June 1997

Contents

Introduction

Meet the members of the new Clue Club. Samantha Scarlet, Peter Plum, Greta Green, and Mortimer Mustard.

These young detectives are all in the same fourth-grade class. The thing they have most in common, though, is their love of mysteries. They formed the Clue Club to talk about mystery books they have read, mystery TV shows and movies they like to watch, and also, to play their favorite game, Clue Jr.

These mystery fans are pretty sharp when it comes to solving real-life mysteries, too. They all use their wits and deductive skills to crack the cases in this book.

You can match *your* wits with this gang of junior detectives to solve the eight mysteries. Can you guess who did it? Check the solution that appears upside down after each story to see if you were right!

The Case
of the Different Fish

"We'll have to have our Clue Club meeting a little late this Saturday," Mortimer Mustard told Peter Plum. "I want to be at the pet store as soon as it opens. The owner, Mrs. Katz, is supposed to be getting some fantail goldfish in anytime and tomorrow might be the day."

"Why don't we just meet you at the pet store?" said Peter. "We can go from there to your house for our meeting."

"Cool," said Mortimer. "I'll call the others."

Bright and early the next morning, Mortimer was standing in front of the Precious Pets Store waiting for Mrs. Katz to open.

"Hey, Mortimer," yelled Greta Green. She came running up with Samantha Scarlet. "Where's Peter?"

"Here I am," shouted Peter, who was half a block behind the girls.

Just then Mrs. Katz opened the door. "Mortimer, you've been here every morning this week when I opened," she laughed. "Well, you're the early bird and today you get the worm. The fantails came in last night, along with some other beauties. Take a look." She pointed to the back of the store where one whole wall was lined with fish tanks.

Mortimer ran back and peered excitedly into the tanks. The rest of the Clue Club decided to look around the store. Samantha and Greta stopped to look at the birds. Meanwhile, several other kids wandered in to look at some new puppies in the window.

Suddenly, the parrot that Samantha and Greta were looking at started to talk. "Hello! Hello!" the parrot kept saying. "Hello! Hello! I have a name."

"What's your name?" Samantha asked the parrot.

4

"Becky," said the parrot. "Hello! Hello, Becky." Samantha and Greta giggled.

"Look at this!" exclaimed Peter, who was a couple of cages down. "A baby ferret. Isn't it great?" The kids looking at the puppies ran over to see the ferret.

Mortimer was still carefully looking at the fish tanks trying to make his choice. Most of the fantails were a solid reddish-orange but two were different. There was an orange one with black speckles across its back and sides that looked almost like a saddle. The other one was silver with reddish-gold markings around the eyes. "I like these," Mortimer told Mrs. Katz, pointing to the two different fish. "The markings make them special." Mrs. Katz scooped the two fish into a bowl and brought them to the counter.

Some other kids had noticed the new fantails and were now peering into the fish tank. "See?" Mortimer told the Clue Club kids. "I told you I had to be here when the store opened. Look at all the kids looking at the fish. They would have gotten mine, I know it."

Mortimer paid for his fish while Mrs. Katz put them in separate containers for him to take home. "Oh, I almost forgot," Mortimer said. "I need fish food. Help me find this special kind. It's called Mermaid Munchies."

Mortimer and the rest of the Clue Club looked along the whole shelf but they couldn't find the Mermaid Munchies. Finally, Mrs. Katz walked back from behind the counter to help them. "Here's one," she said, pulling a box from the back of the top shelf. "They're in the wrong spot."

When they returned to the counter to pay for the fish food, Mortimer noticed that there was only one fish container there. He opened up the box to find the silver fantail. "The black-speckled fantail is gone!" he cried.

"Oh, dear," said Mrs. Katz. "Several people have been looking at the new fish now,

so it's hard to tell who might have taken it. Don't worry, Mortimer, I'll order more. You can have first pick of them for free."

"We'll have some pizza later, Mortimer," said Peter. "That will make you feel better." Mortimer nodded sadly and trudged out the door after the others.

After the Clue Club meeting, the kids headed to the pizza parlor. Fergie Frost and Alice Auburn came in while the kids were eating. Both of them had goldfish containers and they went over to the table to talk to Mortimer about fish.

"I got a black molly today," Fergie told everyone.

Mortimer told them about his black-speckled fantail being taken off the counter. "And after I paid for it, too!" he wailed.

"Too bad," said Fergie. "I wish I'd seen that one first. I'd have bought it for sure."

"My mom got me a black-speckled fantail in Hobart today," Alice said. "We went to Precious Pets first but there weren't any I wanted in the new batch of fish."

Mortimer perked up at the news that the pet store in Hobart had black-speckled fantails. "Hey, I'll ask my mom to take me there tomorrow to see if they have any more."

"Don't bother," Alice said. "There aren't any more."

Mortimer's face dropped again. "Well, I think I'll go anyway and see if they have any that are different," he said.

"Why go all the way over to Hobart?" Alice said. "At least you have the silver one. That's different."

"That's true," Mortimer said. "And the silver one is really special."

"You got a silver fantail?" said Fergie, amazed. "You really scored today."

"Well, I'm going to order some pizza," said Alice. She turned and started toward the counter.

Suddenly Samantha looked at Alice. "Wait a minute, Alice," she said. "You didn't get your black-speckled fantail in Hobart."

9

"Then where did I get it?" Alice said.

"At the Precious Pets Store," answered
Samantha. "You took Mortimer's fish."

How does Samantha know Alice
took Mortimer's fish?

SOLUTION
The Case of the Different Fish

"Oh, yeah? Prove it," Alice retorted.

"Here's my proof," said Samantha. "You knew Mortimer had a silver fantail."

"So what?" said Alice.

"You couldn't have known Mortimer had a silver fantail unless you came into Precious Pets and opened up the containers that held the fish," said Samantha.

"That's right," said Peter. "Mortimer never said he had a silver one."

"And no one else saw the fish in the store but me and Mrs. Katz," said Mortimer.

"You opened the two containers to find the fish you wanted to take," said Greta.

"Alice," exclaimed Mortimer. "I can't believe you'd do this to another fish lover."

"It's just that the fish was so different, Mortimer," sighed Alice. "I'll bring it back to you this afternoon."

"Well, I'm glad to hear that, at least," huffed Mortimer.

"Maybe your mother really *will* take you to Hobart to find a black-speckled fantail," said Samantha.

"Then you'll have a different fish story to tell," laughed Greta.

The Case
of the Karate Chop

It was Thursday. School was out and everyone on the playground was discussing the new karate movie that was opening the coming Saturday. It starred Woo Sun, a fourteen-year-old karate whiz. The Clue Club kids couldn't wait to see it—especially Greta, who took karate classes.

"Be prepared to stand in line," sighed Mortimer. "That's the problem with going on the weekend."

"Well, that's the only time we can go," said Peter. "We have school."

"There's a special matinee tomorrow, but my parents won't let me go during the week," said Samantha.

"Me, either," said Greta. "My mom would kill me if I missed any school. Especially to see a karate movie!"

"Who cares if we have to stand in line?" exclaimed Samantha. "Mortimer, you're too lazy."

"Just think, after you stand in line you can get popcorn and candy!" laughed Peter.

That made Mortimer feel a little better.

Just then Greta spotted Kevin Klear, who was in her karate class. "Kevin!" she shouted. He trotted over. "Want to see the new Woo Sun movie this weekend with us?" Greta asked.

"I can't," Kevin answered.

"Why not?" Greta asked.

"I have to go to my grandmother's all weekend," he replied.

"Too bad," said Greta. "In our karate class Saturday morning, Mr. Lee is going to show us some of the moves Woo Sun does."

"Great," Kevin said, rolling his eyes. "I'll miss that, too."

"There's something coming up that I'd

like to miss," said Peter. "Tomorrow we have our last big science test."

"Plus we're supposed to give our oral book reports tomorrow," Samantha said. Ms. Redding's fourth-grade class was giving group book reports. The students were supposed to act the parts of various characters in each book. "Kevin, Peter, and I are doing *Charlie and the Chocolate Factory*," Samantha told Greta and Mortimer.

The next day at lunch the Clue Club kids were firming up their movie plans. Most of Greta's karate class was going, too: Pauline Pine, Melissa Matte, Frank Flat, Albert Ash, Virgil Vivid, and Willard Wan.

"Why don't we meet at your karate school, Greta?" said Mortimer. "Most of the kids in your class are going anyway."

"Speaking of my karate class, where's Kevin?" asked Greta.

"I heard he was sick," said Mortimer.

"That means Peter and I can't give our book report today. We'll have to go in after

15

school to do it when Kevin comes back. What a bummer," said Samantha.

"Listen, guys, Melissa and I should meet you at the theater," said Pauline. "We have a dance class that morning right after karate."

"My cousin from Hobart and a bunch of kids from his karate class are coming, too," said Albert. "They're also going to meet us at the theater."

"Hey, the place is going to be full of karate kids!" exclaimed Greta.

Monday morning before school started, the playground was full of kids talking about the movie. Everyone was making kicks and chops and imitating Woo Sun's moves. Kevin was even wearing his karate uniform.

"Remember that neat kick Woo Sun did?" Greta said, doing a whirl.

"How did he do that double chop?" asked Pauline. "I've never seen him do that before."

"Like this," said Frank, waving his hands up, then down.

"No, it was like this," said Kevin, chopping the air with his hands. "See?"

"You're so good, Kevin," said Albert. "How long is it going to take me to get that fast?"

"Keep practicing, Albert," said Pauline.

"So, did you have fun at your grandmother's this weekend, Kevin?" asked Mortimer.

"Yeah, it's great there," said Kevin. "She has a big farm with horses and lots of stuff to do. Even if I didn't get to see the movie with the rest of the karate class, I had a good time."

Just then Mr. Higgins, the school principal, walked up to the kids. "Kevin, I wonder if you brought in a note from your mother saying you were sick Friday," he said.

"Oh, I forgot," said Kevin. "I'll bring it in tomorrow."

"That's okay, we can just call your mother," said Mr. Higgins.

"No, you can't!" said Kevin. "I mean, she's at work."

"We have her work number," said Mr. Higgins. "We can just give her a quick call."

"But the note saying I was sick is at home," said Kevin. "I'll go get it now."

"Relax, Kevin," laughed Mr. Higgins. "It's okay that you forgot the note. We'll just call your mom."

After Mr. Higgins had gone into the school, Greta turned to Kevin. "You may as well tell the truth, Kevin," she told him. "Mr. Higgins is going to find out anyway. You weren't sick on Friday."

"You can't prove that," cried Kevin.

"Yes I can," said Greta.

How does Greta know Kevin wasn't sick?

explained. "And I just couldn't wait another week to see it."

"Well, next time you karate chop school, do it on a day when I'm not doing a project with you," Samantha told him.

SOLUTION
The Case of the Karate Chop

"How did you know Woo Sun's double chop move?" Greta asked Kevin.

"He did it in another movie," said Kevin.

"No, he didn't," said Greta. "Our karate teacher said it was a brand-new move."

"Then you must have seen the movie, Kevin," said Peter. "That's how you knew the move."

"Wait a minute! The only time you could have seen it was at the Friday matinee," said Mortimer.

"Which means you had to skip school," said Samantha. "Which means we now have to do our book report *after* school. Thanks a lot, Kevin!"

Caught in his lie, Kevin admitted he played hooky to see the Woo Sun movie.

"I had to go to my grandmother's," he

The Case
of the Losing Race

Each Saturday the kids had their Clue Club meeting at a different house. This Saturday it was at Samantha's house. The kids had their meeting early because they had a lot to do that day. The Little League was having a big fund-raiser to buy new uniforms. Greta and Peter were running in a relay race.

Many of the stores in town were the team sponsors. They had donated all sorts of great things for the Little League to sell—like baked goods, clothing, and gift certificates. There were also several fifty-fifty raffles. Half the money collected went to the winner of the drawing and the other half went to the Little League.

Events for the kids on the teams included all kinds of races: three-legged, crawling, and hopping. The most exciting event, though, was the relay race. The relay pitted the top two Little League teams against each other. This year, Blueville Sporting Goods Store was donating first and second prizes for the relay race. Each member of the winning team would receive a mitt, and the second-place team members would each get a pair of cleats.

When the Clue Club kids got to the park, they walked around looking at the booths and watching the races. But they were really waiting for the relay race that was being held that afternoon. Peter's team, Blueville Sporting Goods, was racing against the Precious Pets Store, Greta's team.

"Let's have a hot dog," said Mortimer, pointing to the refreshment stand.

"Not until after the race," said Peter. "I can't run too well on a full stomach."

"Well, I'm not running," said Mortimer.

"Be right back." And he walked off toward the refreshment stand. The kids sat down on the ground and began talking.

"Tomorrow is the big opening game of the season," said Greta. "I can't wait. Baseball is my favorite sport, I think."

"That's what you said about soccer," said Samantha.

"Well, I guess it is, too," Greta admitted. "They're all my favorites."

"Who do you think will win the relay?" Samantha asked.

"Blueville Sports, of course," said Greta, frowning. "How can they lose? Scott's on their team." She looked over at Scott Sepia, who was taking off his cleats and putting on his sneakers. "Everyone knows Scott is the fastest runner in school."

"Absolutely," Peter said, grinning at his teammate. Scott looked up from tying his sneakers and shrugged, smiling.

"And I could really use a new mitt," sighed Greta.

"I need one, too," said Peter. "How about you, Scott?"

"I got a new one for my birthday last month," Scott replied. "But it doesn't hurt to have two."

"Say, why did you take off your cleats?" asked Peter.

"Like he needs them," muttered Greta.

"They're too tight. My feet must have grown a foot this year." Scott laughed.

Just then the warning whistle blew. "Let's go," said Peter, jumping up. "The race is beginning in a few minutes." The teams walked to the starting line and the first runners crouched down.

BANG! The shot rang out and the two teams lunged forward. Greta and Peter were the first in the lineups. The runners had to race around a twisting, turning path in the park. First Blueville Sports was ahead, then Precious Pets. No one could tell who would win.

Scott was the last on his team to run. He

grabbed the relay stick and took off like a shot, leaving the other team's runner in the dust. By the time he turned the last curve, Blueville was clearly in the lead. But just as Scott was nearing the finish line, he stumbled and grabbed his ankle. After rubbing it for a few seconds, he got up and began to limp ahead. But not before the runner from Precious Pets dashed across the finish line. Scott came in second, then limped off to a chair beside the refreshment stands.

"Yyyeesssss!" shrieked Greta, grabbing Mortimer. "A new mitt!"

Both the Blueville Sports and Precious Pets teams were stunned. Everyone had expected Blueville to win.

"I don't believe it," moaned Peter. "Scott fell!"

"Let's go see how he's doing," said Samantha, walking toward Scott's chair.

"How's your ankle, Scott?" asked Mortimer.

"I guess I twisted it," he answered. "I'm having a hard time walking on it."

The Blueville Sports team coach came over and wrapped Scott's ankle in a bandage. "That will hold you for a while," the coach told him. "If it swells or really hurts, you should go to a doctor."

"Okay," said Scott. "Thanks."

"You want us to pick up your prize for you?" asked Greta.

"Nah, that's okay," Scott answered. "My parents are going to take me over there in a few minutes."

"Wow, we'd better get going," said Peter, looking at his watch. "Blueville's is going to close pretty soon."

"Yeah. If we don't get our prizes, we won't have them for the big game tomorrow," said Greta.

The Clue Club kids got their bikes and rode over to Blueville Sporting Goods as fast as they could.

"Hello, kids," Mr. Blueville said when

they walked through the store's door. "I guess you're here to collect your prizes, right?" He handed Greta a new mitt. "Peter, go sit down with Scott and try on the cleats." He pointed to the shoe section where Scott was sitting.

"Where are your parents, Scott?" asked Peter, sitting down.

"My folks?" Scott answered. "Oh, they went to pick up something." After trying on a few pairs, Scott and Peter found their sizes.

"Mr. Blueville, these cleats are the right size," Scott said.

"Don't forget to leave a little room to grow," Mr. Blueville told him.

"I did." Scott smiled.

Just then, Scott's sister Sue ran into the store. "There you are," she said. "We couldn't find you after the race so we figured you came here to get your prize. Mom and Dad are outside waiting."

"I'm ready," Scott replied. "Tell them I'll be right out." Mr. Blueville handed him the

shoe box and Scott limped toward the door.

"Wait a minute, Scott," said Peter. "I think you pulled a pretty lousy trick."

"What are you talking about?" said Scott.

"I'm talking about you losing the race," said Peter. "On purpose."

**How does Peter know
Scott cheated?**

SOLUTION
The Case of the Losing Race

"What do you mean, Peter?" asked Mr. Blueville.

"Well, Scott was still at the park when we left, Mr. Blueville," said Peter. "He just twisted his ankle, but he beat us getting here."

"And he lied about his parents driving him here," said Mortimer.

"So how did he get here before us unless he ran?" said Samantha.

"And how could he run if his ankle was injured?" said Greta.

"You mean he's faking his twisted ankle?" Mr. Blueville asked. "But why?"

"He did it so he could win the second prize," said Peter.

"I remember," said Mortimer. "You already have a new mitt but your cleats are too small. You told us before the race."

"So you faked a twisted ankle at the last

moment so you could come in second," said Samantha.

"That way you could get the cleats you wanted," said Greta.

"That stinks, Scott," said Peter. "Our team could have won — and I could've had a new mitt!"

Scott admitted he cheated on the race to get the cleats, and gave them back to Mr. Blueville.

"I'll have to talk with the rec department," said Mr. Blueville. "Mr. Plum may want to disqualify you if you cheated."

"You shouldn't have raced over here to get new cleats," said Mortimer. "Now you've come in last."

The Case
of the Billboard's Revenge

It was early spring; allergy season had hit. Several kids were in the nurse's office with swollen eyes from hay fever. Cal Cinnamon came down with the worst case. His face and hands were swollen and he had a rash. It was so bad, the nurse sent him home.

It was also time for electing class officers for the next year. The contest for class president was a very competitive one. Betty Bay, Craig Cherry, and Cal Cinnamon were running and all of them were working hard to win.

One day after school was over, the Clue Club kids met at the pizza parlor. "Cal went home with allergies yesterday," Peter said. "They must have been pretty bad if he had to go home."

"I'm surprised he did," said Greta. "He's really trying hard to win class president."

"Being sick probably won't slow him down," said Samantha. "Especially since his father is doing everything."

"I think Cal's really nice," said Greta. "He can't help it if his rich father thinks money will buy Cal everything."

"Yeah," agreed Peter. "A lot of other kids really resent him, though."

"That's because of his father," said Samantha. "Cal's trying to win on his own, but his father keeps butting in."

"I'd be embarrassed," said Mortimer, shaking his head. "First Mr. Cinnamon put up flyers all over the whole town for Cal. But the billboard ad was the worst."

"Well, Cal is embarrassed, too," said Greta. "But his father won't take it down. He says it will help Cal win."

"Who do you think painted the mustache on the billboard?" asked Peter. Two days earlier someone had added a mustache to Cal's face on the billboard.

"Probably one of the kids running against Cal for class president," said Samantha.

That morning, the principal, Mr. Higgins, had called a school assembly and brought Cal up onstage. "I'd like to know who is responsible for defacing Cal's billboard," he questioned the students. No one responded.

"The ad will obviously come down," the principal went on. "It's just a shame people can't resist destroying someone else's good fortune. I hate to say this, but I won't be surprised if the culprit is one of the other candidates for class president." Cal blushed through his rash, but the principal kept talking.

"I'm deeply disappointed that the guilty one hasn't come clean," Mr. Higgins said. "I'll always wonder if next year's president is the one who committed this terrible deed just to win the election." Embarrassed, Cal squirmed until Mr. Higgins finally dismissed the assembly.

"I haven't seen the billboard, have you?" Mortimer asked the Clue Club kids. None of them had, so they decided to run over to look at it after school.

When they got there, a park attendant was there pulling weeds. "Don't come over here, kids," he told them. "There's a patch of poison ivy growing up the billboard supports. The good news is I think this is the last bunch growing in town. It's taken me nearly five years but I think I've gotten rid of all of it. All except this."

Suddenly Peter's mouth dropped open. "Wait a minute!" he exclaimed. "I know who painted the mustache on Cal." When he told the others, they nodded their heads in agreement.

The next day the kids went to the principal's office and told him they thought they knew who defaced the billboard. "Could you ask the three candidates running for office and the school nurse to come to my office?" Mr. Higgins told his secretary.

When everyone was assembled, Peter announced that the culprit was Cal.

"Why would I mess up my own billboard and make myself look ridiculous?" Cal cried.

"Do you have some proof to back this up, Peter?" asked Mr. Higgins.

Why does Peter think Cal defaced his own billboard?

SOLUTION
The Case of the Billboard's Revenge

"Yep," answered Peter. "We found out yesterday that the billboard's supports are covered with poison ivy. Anyone climbing up them would come down with an itchy rash and swell up." Everyone looked at Cal.

"Would you say Cal's rash looks like hay fever allergies or poison ivy?" Mr. Higgins asked the nurse.

"Definitely poison ivy," she replied. "That's what I told him when I sent him home."

"Since Cal is the only kid in the room with poison ivy, he's got to be the one who climbed up the billboard supports," Peter said.

"Why did you deface your own billboard, Cal?" asked Mr. Higgins.

"Because now my dad will have to take down the ad," Cal replied.

"You mean you don't want it?" asked Mr. Higgins.

"No!" said Cal. "I want to win the election because I'll do a good job, not because of how much my father can help me."

"I admire you for that, son," said Mr. Higgins. "I'd say you should be punished, but it was your ad, after all."

"Besides, the poison ivy is punishment enough," laughed Greta.

The Case
of the False Alarm

"**P**eter, I have something for you," Mr. Plum called out when he came home from work.

Peter came running down the stairs from his room. "What's up, Dad?" he asked.

Mr. Plum handed Peter some special reflecting tape from the recreation department where he worked. It was a green, gold, and red swirled pattern with silver stars and half-moons on it. "This is for your bike, to make sure cars can see you when you ride in the evenings."

"Cool pattern!" Peter exclaimed.

"I thought you'd like that." His father smiled.

The next day Peter took the tape to school to show everyone in the schoolyard. All the kids wanted to know where they could get some, too. "I'll have to ask my dad," Peter told them.

After school, the Clue Club kids were in Peter's yard, watching him put the tape on his bike.

"Looks like I only have enough for one fender," said Peter. "I'll have to ask Dad to bring home some more."

"Can he bring enough for the whole school?" asked Samantha, laughing. "Everyone loves that pattern."

"I know, it's so cool," said Peter.

"Well, I have to go," said Mortimer. "Time for dinner."

"Mortimer's never late to eat," laughed Greta.

"I'm supposed to be home, too," said Samantha. "See you later, guys."

"Okay," said Peter. "We're meeting for ice cream after dinner, right?"

That evening, the kids met for an ice-cream cone at the Frosty Float. "Yum," said Mortimer, taking a lick. "Nothing like double-fudge chocolate."

The kids sat talking while they finished their ice cream. They discussed what they would do at their Clue Club meeting the next day. That week it was Peter's turn to hold the meeting.

The following morning, Samantha had just finished reading the club minutes from the last meeting when Peter's parents came into Peter's room.

"Peter, the police called," Mr. Plum told him. "They want us to come downtown to the police station."

"How come?" Peter asked.

"Someone has been setting off fire alarms over the last few days and you've been accused," Mrs. Plum said.

"Me?" cried Peter.

"Gordon Glow, a kid from your school, says he saw you setting off an alarm last night," explained Mr. Plum.

"Hey, we were all out together last night," said Greta.

"That's right," said Mr. Plum. "Call your

parents and see if it's all right for you to go with us to the station."

"Good idea," said Mrs. Plum. "We know Peter didn't do this and maybe you guys can help get to the bottom of this mystery."

When they got to the station, Mr. Glow was there with his son. "I knew Gordon was in the same area when a couple of the alarms were set off," he explained to the Plums. "I was beginning to suspect him. Then yesterday evening I saw him riding away from an alarm box on the corner near our house. When the fire trucks showed up, I finally confronted him."

Mr. Glow looked at Peter. "That's when Gordon accused Peter," he said. "He said he saw Peter riding away on his bike after pulling the alarm."

"It's true, Dad," Gordon said. "I was riding after Peter, trying to catch him."

"But Peter was with us," said Mortimer. "We were at the Frosty Float having ice cream."

"I appreciate your coming forward," said Officer Lawford. "But you're Peter's friend. Would you lie for him?"

"Of course he would," exclaimed Gordon. "They all would!"

"How could you tell it was Peter?" asked Mrs. Plum. "After all, it was nighttime and pretty dark."

"Because of his bike," answered Gordon.

"How did you know it was Peter's bike?" Officer Lawford said to Gordon.

"I've seen Peter's bike at school before," answered Gordon.

"Plenty of people have bikes that look like mine," Peter said.

"Can you describe anything about the bike?" Officer Lawford asked Gordon. Gordon nodded his head.

"Definitely," he said. "While I was chasing Peter, I noticed the reflector tape he put on the fender. No one else has that kind. Peter's dad brought it home from the rec department and Peter showed it to us at school. That's how I knew it was Peter's bike."

"Excuse me, Officer Lawford," said Samantha, "but Gordon is lying."

How does Samantha know Gordon is lying?

After getting caught in a lie, Gordon finally confessed to having pulled several false alarms. The police told the Plums they could go home.

"Well, I'm glad you children got that false charge cleared up," said Mrs. Plum.

"That reflector tape has saved me in more ways than one, Dad," laughed Peter.

SOLUTION
The Case of the False Alarm

"Gordon never saw the reflector tape on Peter's bike," said Samantha.

"Sure I did," said Gordon. "It's green and red and gold with silver stars and half-moons on it."

"You saw the tape at school when Peter brought it in, but you didn't see it on his bike," said Greta. "You couldn't have."

"Why not?" asked Officer Lawford.

"Because Gordon could only have seen the back of Peter's bike," said Mortimer.

"What do you mean?" asked Gordon.

"Peter only put the tape on his front fender," said Samantha. "He didn't have enough for the back one."

"Of course," said Peter. "There's no way Gordon could have seen the tape if he was chasing me from behind."

"So what is the truth, son?" Officer Lawford asked Gordon.

6

The Case of the Bad Name

Peter hung up the phone and immediately dialed Greta. "We've got a case," he announced. "You call Samantha and I'll call Mortimer. Meet me at my house right away and I'll tell you what's up."

"Right-o," said Greta.

In no time the other Clue Club kids were at Peter's, ready to solve a mystery.

"So what's up?" said Greta.

"Here's the deal," Peter explained. "Mr. Coffee poured a patch of cement at the curb in front of his house."

"How come?" asked Mortimer.

"So he can have a flat surface to sit his garbage can on," giggled Peter. The kids burst out laughing.

"Everything has to be just so for him,"

laughed Greta, holding her stomach. "Ray Lime cut his grass once and Mr. Coffee fired him because it was uneven."

"What does this have to do with the case?" asked Samantha.

"Well, Mr. Coffee poured the cement last night so it would be dry by this morning," continued Peter. "Sometime last night, someone wrote her name in it."

"What do you mean someone?" asked Greta. "Who was it?"

"Well, no one knows for sure," said Peter. "Either Alexis Lime or Allana Azure."

"That doesn't make any sense," said Samantha. "Whose name is in the concrete?"

"I don't know," admitted Peter. "Alexis called me this morning and asked if we could help her figure out what's going on."

"I'm confused," said Greta.

"Well then, let's go see if we can figure this out!" said Mortimer, jumping up.

When the kids arrived at Alexis's house, she told them she was just leaving to go to a baseball game.

"Just tell us what happened before you go," said Peter. "Quick."

"Okay," said Alexis, coming out onto the porch. "Mr. Coffee called my parents this morning. He says either Allana or I wrote our name in his cement."

"So who was it?" asked Mortimer.

"It wasn't me!" Alexis snapped. "But I'm grounded now because of it. I can't go anywhere except to baseball until this gets cleared up."

"But what name is in the concrete?" asked Mortimer. "Alexis or Allana?"

"I don't know. I haven't seen the concrete," Alexis said. "I can't even go out to look at it. That's why I called you guys. You know how to solve mysteries. Well, here's one for you."

"I guess we'll go talk to Allana," said Peter. "We'll see you later."

The kids walked around the corner to

see Allana, who was also grounded. "Alexis did this," Allana said angrily. "She's just lying so she won't get in trouble. But now *I'm* in trouble."

"She's no help, either," said Greta after they left. "I guess we should go look at the concrete."

They arrived just as Mr. Coffee was getting ready to mix up some more cement to patch over the name. Written on the sidewalk in large letters was *ALLIE WAS HERE*.

"I see what the problem is," said Peter. "Whoever did it wrote her nickname in the cement, not her full first name."

"They both have the same nickname," said Samantha. "How are we going to be able to tell who wrote this?"

"Wait a minute!" exclaimed Greta. "I know!" She walked over to Mr. Coffee. "I can show you who wrote the name," she said. "But you have to wait until this afternoon to redo your patch. Okay?"

"No!" Mr. Coffee said grumpily. "Oooh, all right. If you're sure you can do it."

"I can," said Greta confidently. "Okay, guys, let's go watch Alexis's baseball game."

The kids biked over to the baseball field. Alexis was sitting glumly on the bench in her warm-up jacket.

"If you and your parents will come over to Mr. Coffee's house after the game, we can show them who wrote in the concrete," Greta told her.

"Sounds good," said Alexis, brightening up. "We'll be there. Now watch me hit a home run."

After the game Greta told Alexis, "Meet us at Mr. Coffee's. We have one stop to make first."

"Now where?" asked Mortimer.

"To get Allana," said Greta. The kids told Allana and her parents to meet them at Mr. Coffee's and they would solve the mystery of the name.

"Great!" said Allana. "Maybe now I'll get out of the doghouse."

When Allana and Alexis and their parents arrived at Mr. Coffee's front yard, Greta announced who wrote in the cement.

"It was Allana," she said.

"What?" shouted Allana. "Wait a minute. How can you tell? We both have the same nickname. There's no way you can prove who did it."

"I don't have to," said Greta. "You did."

How does Greta know Allana wrote her name in the concrete?

SOLUTION
The Case of the Bad Name

"What do you mean, I did?" said Allana.

"I mean you wrote your name, not Alexis's," said Greta. "Look at it."

Everyone looked down at the cement. "Oh, I see what you mean, Greta," said Alexis, laughing.

"I do, too," said Peter. Samantha and Mortimer nodded their heads.

"Spell your nickname, Allana," said Greta.

"A-L-L-I-E," said Allana. "What's the deal?"

"Alexis, turn around and show Allana the back of your jacket," said Samantha.

When Alexis turned around, Allana saw her nickname written on the back of her jacket — ALIE. "Oh," said Allana.

"See, Allana?" Alexis said. "I spell my nickname a different way than you do."

"You didn't know that or you wouldn't have tried to blame Alexis," said Mortimer.

"Oh, I just couldn't resist the wet concrete," confessed Allana. "I thought neither one of us would get into trouble if no one could figure out who did it. But we both got into trouble. I'm sorry I ruined your concrete, Mr. Coffee."

"Shame on you for trying to give Alexis a bad name, Allana," said Mr. Coffee, smoothing fresh cement over the words. "Maybe you can help me fix the square for my garbage can now."

"Greta cleared Alexis's name, Mr. Coffee," said Mortimer, laughing. "Now it's up to Allana to smooth things over."

The Case
of the Extra Clue

"**A**ttention!" Rex Rouge called out to the kids at his birthday party. "We're going to have a treasure hunt. Everybody divide up into two teams."

"Oh, cool!" exclaimed Greta. "I love treasure hunts."

"Each team has a different map," Rex told his guests. "You'll find a clue at each of the spots marked on the map. Put all the clues together, and they will lead you to the treasure. Whoever brings that item back to the house first wins the prize." Then Rex brought out two maps — one for each team.

"These maps are cool," said Mortimer. "They look old."

"Thanks," beamed Rex. "I used a special

fountain pen and brown ink to make the maps look old."

"Can I see the pen?" Mortimer asked.

"Sure," said Rex. "I put it up on the shelf." But when he looked for the pen, he couldn't find it.

"Hmm. It's gone now," said Rex. "My mom might have put it away so nobody would start playing with it and get ink all over everything. It leaks, so you have to be really careful when you use it. The ink's permanent. Look, I scrubbed my hands three times, trying to get the ink off, and there's still some left." He showed Mortimer his right hand, which had dirty-looking stains on the fingers.

Mike Manila grabbed one of the maps. "Let's get going," he said.

"Take it easy," laughed Rex.

"I just want to get started," Mike said.

"Yeah," said Martha Mudd, who was on Mike's team. "I've never been on a treasure hunt before."

After the teams studied their maps for a

minute, they took off in different directions. All the Clue Club kids were on one team. At each stop they figured out the clues quickly, except for the last one. After searching for a while, the Clue Club kids gave up and went back to the house.

When they arrived, the other team was already there. They had found the treasure.

"I guess you guys won the prize," said Peter.

"What took you so long?" asked Rex.

"We couldn't find the last clue," said Samantha.

"Did you look inside?" asked Martha.

"Inside what?" said Samantha.

"The mailbox," answered Mike.

"The mailbox wasn't on the map," said Samantha.

"Yes it was," said Rex, taking the map.

Mortimer looked over Rex's shoulder.

"Wow," Rex said to Mortimer. "The last clue on your map says to go fifteen steps from the front porch steps. Let's try it."

The kids walked fifteen steps from the porch steps and found themselves at the curb. "Some one must have changed your map. It should be five steps to the mailbox."

"Who would do that?" asked Greta.

"It's a real mystery," said Martha.

Just then Rex's mom called to the kids to wash up for cake and ice cream.

"Mmmm, just look at you boys," she said looking at Rex and Mike. "I should send you both back to wash your dirty hands. Oh, well. Go ahead and have some cake."

After everyone sang "Happy Birthday," Rex blew out the candles in one breath. Mrs. Rouge heaped a huge scoop of ice cream on top of each piece of cake.

"I'm surprised that you didn't win," said Rex between bites. "I know that I wrote five steps. I double-checked all the clues."

"Someone in the winning group cheated," said Samantha.

Suddenly Mortimer put down his fork. "I think I know who it was," he said.

"Who?" said Samantha.

"Mike," said Mortimer, pointing at him with his fork.

"Me?" said Mike. "Why me?"

"Two clues," replied Mortimer.

How does Mortimer know Mike changed the map?

SOLUTION
The Case of the Extra Clue

"The first clue is your dirty hands," said Mortimer, pushing up his glasses.

"Dirty hands don't make me a map changer," said Mike.

"Wait a minute. That's not dirt, it's brown ink!" shouted Rex, looking closely at his hand then Mike's.

"I guess some of it smeared on my hand when I grabbed the map," Mike said.

"I think you got ink smeared on you when you changed our map," said Mortimer.

"You can't prove that," said Mike. "Maybe I just picked up the pen and it leaked on me."

"You're right," said Mortimer. "But that's where the second clue comes in."

"Go, Mortimer!" exclaimed Greta.

"When we told everyone we couldn't find the last clue, you asked if we looked inside," Mortimer reminded Mike. "How did you know we could look inside the last place we went?"

"Unless you added it to the map?" cried Samantha.

"Okay, I changed the map," Mike confessed. "I didn't think anyone would notice."

"You forgot there are great detectives here," said Peter.

"You don't get any prize then," said Rex. "You're lucky I'm going to let you keep your cake."

"I guess that'll teach Mike not to mess with the mail," snickered Greta.

The Case
of the Wrong Floor

The Clue Club kids were delighted to find out that Jenny Jewel, the new kid in fourth grade, was also a mystery lover. One day Jenny invited the Clue Club kids to her house. "I'll show you my collection of mystery movies," she told them.

The next Saturday, after their weekly Clue Club meeting, the kids headed off to visit Jenny. She lived on the very top floor of the new sixteen-story apartment building in town. When the kids arrived at the building, a very dignified doorman greeted them.

"Whom are you coming to see?" the doorman asked them.

"Jenny Jewel," Peter told him.

"And who shall I say is here?" the doorman said.

"The Clue Club," said Greta.

"Very good," the doorman said, smiling. He reached for the intercom and called Jenny's apartment. " The Clue Club is here to see you," he told her.

After he hung up he told the kids, "Jenny says she'll wait for you in front of the elevator. You may go up now." He nodded toward the elevators in the lobby behind him.

"Thank you," said Samantha as the kids went to the elevator.

"Hey, guys!" said Jenny when the elevator door opened on the top floor. "Come on in."

The kids ran to the living room windows as soon as they were inside Jenny's apartment. "Wow!" exclaimed Greta. "Check out this view."

"We're above the trees," cried Samantha.

"This is even better than my tree house," said Peter.

Jenny hauled out her collection of mystery movies and books. "I even have copies of some old TV mystery shows," she told them. "But they're still in the basement in storage."

"Hey, we'll help you bring them up, if you want," offered Peter.

"That would be great," said Jenny. "Then we could watch some."

As they were waiting for the elevator, Jenny's next-door neighbor came out of his apartment. The elderly man was trying to carry two trash bags.

"Hi, Mr. Goldfarb," said Jenny. She introduced the kids to him. "Here. We'll take your trash to the chute for you," she told him.

"Thank you, children," Mr. Goldfarb said, handing the bags over. "It's a little hard to carry two things. I need one hand for my cane."

Mortimer noticed that Mr. Goldfarb's cane had an unusual handle. It was the shape of a cat's head.

"That's a cool cane," Mortimer told him.

"Thank you, son," he says. "The cat shape is also easy to grip."

After Mr. Goldfarb had gone inside, the kids pushed the elevator button to go downstairs.

"I first met Mr. Goldfarb in the lobby," Jenny told them while they waited. "He likes to sit there and talk to everyone in the building. I guess it's because he lives by himself and he gets lonely."

"What are your other neighbors like?" asked Greta.

"A painter lives on the other side of us," said Jenny. "He painted a picture of our dog once, but it didn't look anything like Foxy." Finally, Jenny pointed to the last apartment at the end of the hall. "Three college students live there. And that's my neighborhood!" she laughed. "Now let's go find my videos."

When they reached the lobby, Jenny found Mr. Broom, the superintendent of the building. She explained that they wanted to get a couple of boxes she had in storage. "Come on, then," Mr. Broom said. "I'll take you to the basement. I think I know right where your things are, Jenny."

When Mr. Broom opened the basement door, it startled a kid who was going through some storage boxes.

"Who are you?" asked Mr. Broom. "And what are you doing down here?"

"Trevor Toast," the kid told him. "I'm visiting my aunt. She lives in 16-A. She's been keeping some things of mine for me and I just came down to get them."

"You should have asked me to come with you," said Mr. Broom. "No one is allowed down here without my permission."

"Sorry. My aunt didn't tell me that," said Trevor. "She's kind of old and forgetful. I guess I'll go back upstairs and ask her if she can remember exactly where everything is."

"Well, if you wait a couple of minutes, I'll help you find your things," said Mr. Broom. "Let me take care of these kids first." He looked around. "I'll be right back," he said, walking into a back room. "I want to get my flashlight."

"Tell the super that's okay," Trevor told the kids. "I'll just hop on the elevator and ask my aunt if my stuff is really here." He turned and walked toward the elevator.

"Wait a minute," Mortimer told the kid. "Samantha, go get Mr. Broom. I don't think Trevor is down here looking for his things."

"Oh, no?" said Trevor.

"No," said Mortimer. "I think you're looking for other people's things."

How does Mortimer know Trevor is lying?

"No one else lives on the sixteenth floor, right, Jenny?" said Mortimer.

"That's right," replied Jenny. "You guys are good at solving mysteries. I didn't even think of that."

"Well, I think we'll call security," said Mr. Broom.

"It looks like you picked the wrong floor to move your made-up aunt to, Trevor," said Peter.

SOLUTION
The Case of the Wrong Floor

Mr. Broom returned with Samantha. "What's going on?" he asked.

"Trevor isn't telling you the truth," Mortimer told him.

"How do you know, son?" asked Mr. Broom.

"You said your aunt lives on the sixteenth floor in 16-A, right?" Mortimer asked Trevor.

"Right," said Trevor.

"Wrong," said Mortimer.

"Oh, yeah," said Greta. "Jenny lives on the sixteenth floor."

"I see what you mean, Mortimer," said Samantha. "Jenny told us about all her neighbors."

"Besides Jenny and her mom, there is Mr. Goldfarb, the painter, and the three college students. That's it," said Peter.

Your favorite game is a mystery series!

created by
Parker C. Hinter

Samantha Scarlet, Peter Plum, Greta Green and Mortimer Mustard need your help! If you like playing the game Clue™ Jr., you'll love helping the Clue™ Jr. Kids solve the mysteries in these great books!

❏ BBJ47907-5	#1	The Case of the Secret Message	$2.95
❏ BBJ47908-3	#2	The Case of the Stolen Jewel	$2.99
❏ BBJ26217-3	#3	The Case of the Chocolate Fingerprints	$2.99
❏ BBJ26218-1	#4	The Case of the Missing Movie	$2.99
❏ BBJ62372-9	#5	The Case of the Zoo Clue	$2.99
❏ BBJ62373-7	#6	The Case of the Runaway Turtle	$2.99
❏ BBJ86633-8	#7	The Case of the Mystery Ghost	$2.99
❏ BBJ86634-6	#8	The Case of the Clubhouse Thief	$3.50
❏ BBJ86635-4	#9	The Case of the Karate Chop	$3.50

Available wherever you buy books...or use this order form.

Scholastic Inc., P.O. Box 7502, 2931 E. McCarty Street, Jefferson City, MO 65102-7502

Please send me the books I have checked above. I am enclosing $_____ (please add $2.00 to cover shipping and handling). Send check or money order — no cash or C.O.D.s please.

Name _____ Birthdate _____

Address _____

City_____ State/Zip _____

Please allow four to six weeks for delivery. Offer good in the U.S. only. Sorry, mail orders are not available to residents of Canada. Prices subject to change. CLJR1196